CW01574455

To/

Leo and Gina,

Wishing you all the very best for the future, and much happiness in the Rugby Club and all you do.

Cheers!

Joan xxx

alais Louise Walker.

BLACKBERRY AND APPLE

Louise Walker

MINERVA PRESS
LONDON
MONTREUX LOS ANGELES SYDNEY

BLACKBERRY AND APPLE

ISBN 1 86106 928 6

First Published 1997 by
MINERVA PRESS
195 Knightsbridge
London SW7 1RE

Printed in Great Britain for Minerva Press

BLACKBERRY AND APPLE

I dedicate this book to my lovely grandson, Sam, who was so interested in the War, that he started me telling him this! He liked my chronicles for bedtime stories.

Contents

In 1939, just before the War, a family of four move from London to the country, to be safer. They all 'do their bit', as the saying goes, from there. This story is a glimpse from childhood, set in a village, with loving animals, of all the fun experienced in those remarkable five years. The dark and the light like blackberry and apple!

Chapter One

Country Home

Heavy pale green Chintz lounge covers, a cream plate of corned beef, mash and home-made chutney, or a horse's black leather bridle – takes me back to our country home in the War. Lovely reminders of those exceptional five years.

Our haven was a square, whitewashed bungalow, tucked back between a row of fairly new council houses. There was a long drive up to it, from which our white gate displayed the name 'Ringwood', and all that we had for sale. This consisted of our home-grown vegetables and salad stuff, chickens, rabbits, eggs and the cars that my father had reconditioned. For the latter, he had built a double garage, and from there we had the chance to drive in a Daimler taxi and all sorts of old luxurious saloons! We would never have normally had the opportunity to be owners of such cars, so it was great fun to try them out when my father was giving them a test run! People could not afford to keep them in the War – nor was there the petrol allowance to warrant them – so Dad sold them to a few of the exceptions. It was fun weighing up the potatoes or tomatoes for the callers, and collecting the freshly laid eggs. It was quite a different existence from our London life, and made us laugh humping a pile of wet, muddy cabbages about, up to our chins!

The War started, and under these dark clouds – as Churchill put it – we all drew closer together, in one common cause – to 'overcome the oppressor, Hitler'! The courageous British humour helped us through, conquering what seemed the impossible then! Our tiny island, in such peril, rose to the occasion, with our brave soldiers (called Tommies), our daring airmen (called Wizard Prangs) and indomitable sailors (called Sailor Blues) showing incredible strength of character. It was our 'finest hour', as Winston Churchill predicted, when we won five years later! He would drive in a tank or walk about visiting his troops in the front line, to encourage them. On land, sea or air, he urged them to victory, by his V for victory sign with his fingers in mid-air! It caught on, and then everyone was doing it. He also puffed on his big cigar, wherever he went.

During this time, from 1939 to 1945, we were just an ordinary London family moving to the heart of the country for safety, but still to do 'our bit', as they said. Wherever you lived you were just as important to help. We did a lot of 'Digging for Victory', as the slogan went on the posters, by working on our land for very long hours. All very healthy and worthwhile. My father also belonged to the home guard. What a scream! Just like *Dad's Army* on the television now. My mother looked after ten evacuees besides our family. Marie, who was six at the outbreak of War, and I nine, helped with most jobs going on and also knitted balaclavas for the army. They asked us to pin a card with a message on inside them, together with our name. We often wondered who got our efforts, which we hoped kept them warm in cold countries where they fought.

The best treat of living in the country was to have our two black Labrador dogs! They were lively and so loving - but often got into scrapes with the local farmers, when they got out and chased their cows or pigs! We also had two cats, three kittens, two pet rabbits, and twenty rabbits to sell, four horses and a donkey. They were all lovely and a whole new interest for us. We had to learn how to care for them all properly, whilst grooming and feeding them too. They smelled wonderful - all really clean, as Dad did everything thoroughly - especially when it was sunny after the rain. It brought out the natural smells and we would pat or stroke their coats, and wander around in the warm sweet hay. The sacks of potatoes and peas, stacked in a corner, would give off earthy aromas. Fresh green tangs arose from the cabbages and greens of all kinds, together with fresh apples and marrows. The dusty, muddy life around the stables, was enhanced by the strong smelling hides of the gleaming horses, and their harness tack hanging on the walls. Crunching and munching, as they ate from the hay bars, and stomped on the straw. Added to this were lovely country sounds of the birds singing, and the bees hovering around the larkspur.

My mother's flowers were flourishing all around the bungalow and down the little paths. There was a large bed in the front, that sloped from a high bank of hollyhocks down to little forget-me-nots at the border. Dad had dotted barrels of cypress trees around the front windows, and laid a large expanse of new concrete up to the double garage. The back garden had a thick lawn surrounded by laurel bushes. On the left stood our two playhouses, built by Dad, with pretty rustic porches. Out of reject pit props my father made six large greenhouses, four stables, and two long workshops. These were situated beyond the back garden, where there were also rabbit hutches, chicken coops and glass frames, amongst a little orchard. High up on the left the land swept up to a spinney, where we had our swings. There were two fields to the right, where potatoes and peas grew and then another large potato field across the farm lane from them. Along the edges of these fields grew large flat mushrooms, which we could gather in the September dew.

Our great Auntie Beckie sat bolt upright in the leather tub chair at home, and crocheted hats and bags for the whist drive prizes. She also helped prepare the string beans, and other such vegetables for dinner. The lounge in which she sat was a long room with a large bow window, furnished in heavy pale green chintz all round, with a pewter courtier stove at the end. Most of our family life took place in there, including parties and dart games. Dinner was eaten round the big dark oak dining room table, and studded leather chairs. This was flanked by all the Jacobean suite of sideboard, desk and bookcase to match it. Standing majestically by was the grandfather clock. Dark oak figuring around the shiny brass face, with brass pendulum and weights, it looked very similar to the suite, and added to the Jacobean theme at the dining end of the family room. Even with all this heavy furniture and large lounge suite there was plenty of walking room; which was just as well, with so many of us living there during the War. Of course, all fourteen of us were not there all together most of the time – and Marie and I had our tea in the hall, which was just like a room on board ship! It was in a circular shape having doors all designed with a porthole effect on them. It was dark with no windows, but the bright red Turkish carpet cheered it up, together with the cream gloss paintwork. There was a dark oak Windsor set in there, which was ideally light and spacious for us crossing the room, from door to door. We all managed, and fitted in happily by keeping to a clockwork routine.

The Jewish families who stayed, were charming, and we loved them living with us. They had been bombed out from London raids, and fled to the country. We were lucky having them, as they were exceptional people, who gave Marie and I a taste of smart adult life.

They dressed very well, in tailored or pleated outfits, with beautiful blouses or fancy knit jumpers. They were generous and even gave us some of the latter. Mine, from a gorgeous girl called Nula, who came when she was on leave from the WRNS - was a banana fleck wool, with an all over loopy pattern. I was thrilled. Marie's was from her favourite, called Vita, of the ATS, in pale pink with silky strands in it. This gave Marie immense pleasure as it was so glamorous. The whole family were always so generous and sophisticated quite unlike any others we had met. Being Jewish, they liked fish cooked in olive oil - and even the actual olives in a salad: quite usual today, but at that time we had never tried such tasters. They had beautiful complexions and glorious bouncy hair - possibly from them! It was agony to hear what might have happened to these Jews if they had been in Europe. Horrific tales began to seep across from there, about their tortures. When we looked in their eves, it seemed unbelievable that anyone could do such terrible things to those such as our friends here. Oh bitter, dark horrors of this world War.

The London Blitz was on - the colossal burning from the German bombs. We could see the sky lit up in bright orange - sixty miles away from it! Days of deep intent, and of utmost importance to our future freedom - like the plough leaving a furrow in the soil.

Chapter Two

Amusing Happenings

A funny thing happened one day when I was at my friend's cottage. Paddy's mother, named Germaine, was standing in the little passage leading to the kitchen. She was a handsome, dark-haired lady from Gibraltar, wearing a navy jumper and full-flowing flowered skirts, pottering away making tea.

Suddenly the teaspoons clattered and she shrieked. A mouse had run up under her skirts! We were thunder struck – watching the sight. Then Paddy got a rolled newspaper and tried to hit it. It would not go away! Germaine screamed and screamed, dashing from one side to another. Her husband Patrick was still frozen on the settee. It took so long for the mouse to run off we couldn't believe it. Germaine angrily strode over to Patrick.

"Why didn't you do something?" she cried.

The big volatile Irishman was white and silent for once! Then Paddy had hysterics.

Eventually they calmed down, and Germaine refused to make tea that day!

Our strawberry roan, Dandy, was a lively little colt. He tripped smartly around pulling the black and gold trap. One day, when our family of four were out with Dandy, a wasp stung his haunches. Immediately he kicked his back legs and then bolted. His hooves hammered the floor of the trap. Either from pain – or enjoyment of the banging noise, he continued, completely ignoring my father's commands to stop! On and on we swayed, until tearing round a bend in the lane we saw a group of children in our path! Dad told us to hold tight or jump if we had to because he must save the children. He stood up again, and pulled with all his might, while trying to quieten him. Dad tugged to the right and over went the trap. We flew in the air and landed with a crash.

Mum and Marie managed to reach the grass verge, I was half on and half off the loose gravel road, and cut my head and cheek, whilst Dad came over the top of me – as I looked up – and fell onto a driveway and broke his arm. Dandy came to a jerking halt with the twisted shafts of the trap digging in him. He was steaming with white froth on his pounding body, while his poor eyes were flashing around. He tossed his head and made loud snorting noises, whilst we slowly got up from the ground. The 'well-to-do' lady from the nearby house came out and welcomed us into her kitchen to be bathed. Later I had three stitches in my head, and grit taken out of my cheek, and then Mum, Marie and I were all right.

The next day, Dad had to go to hospital and sat for hours in the waiting room. They decided he must have his arm set, and an injection against tetanus or lock jaw. Eventually the nurses came and apologised to him – they had given his injection to the man sitting next to him by mistake! Dad had questioned them several times but, they assured him it wouldn't be long each time! How Dad laughed – the poor chap had only come in for some ointment, he told him.

The vicar of our little village stood six feet tall, with a white pointed beard and tufted white hair. He looked 'for all the world' just like his twelve white goats! They rambled about his large vicarage garden devouring all sorts! We could watch them from our adjoining school playground. He was an eccentric professor type – a very scholarly man – pronouncing his sermons with a flash of the white surplice and his hands appearing again to be clasped in prayer! He quoted in Latin, chanted in a sweet pious voice, and checked on his notes peering through half glasses on the end of his nose. A wonderfully dramatic performance every matins I attended.

He guided me through my confirmation classes – which, on many occasions, I wondered if I would ever receive his approval to pass – but I did. I must say, he always looked so regal and thoroughly absorbed, that I felt a tinge of fond admiration as I watched him with the Bishop at my confirmation. All his wonderful words, like unction, corpus Christi, Holy Spirit of the Trinity, and Seraphim all became understandable; I was remembering what he had said, to the thunderous organ music. Uplifting and unforgettable, it confirmed my true belief and has remained with me ever since. The dainty gold cross and chain, given to me that day by my godmother, reminds me of how frail and faint I felt on going in. Even though my beautiful white and silver cobweb patterned dress, made by my mother, was so comforting, I was ill at ease. It was a chill day, and I shivered - as did we all. The whole scene in the cold stone church, made me tremble with apprehension. I need not have felt so troubled at all! The service was compelling, and I was soon singing and looking at the coloured stain glassed windows. The Bishop looked wonderful, and our vicar seemed to ‘come to life’ here. I was really pleased he was unusual; and realised how lucky we were to have such a character in our midst.

Country life had as many twists and turns as our country lanes. Delightfully rustic, with academic overtones!

Chapter Three

The Dinner Lady

Mince and dumplings bubbling merrily in a pot, Savoy cabbage boiling away, it's just like on the school canteen cooker in the War. The appetising wafts send me back to when my Auntie Cora was the village school dinner lady. What tasty dinners she made - all on her own, for about thirty children peeling all the carrots and potatoes etc. herself.

She worked away patiently in the dull back kitchen, which had no view, just an ugly tree in a small yard, enclosed by an old brick wall. At least a few birds would come and sit on the tree in the summer. Never-the-less she was happy every day.

Cora loved the children coming in so eagerly for their meal. She made it very satisfying even though there was the food rationing, all meat, fats, sugar and powdered egg were allocated, so the fresh vegetables helped. Being in the country, and by digging for victory, like ourselves, there was more available. Cora dished up menus that were popular with the children. Nearly every day they would clear the lot!

The teachers would walk the pupils in a 'crocodile' from the school, about fifty yards away. This canteen was a converted chapel. It was a lovely character place for them to come for dinner. It had a very high window with stone sills, and ropes for opening the flap, oak panelled walls, and flagstone floor. The sound of scraping on the floor when they sat down at the long trestle tables, and their general mischievous noises - were loud!

Auntie Cora was tiny, with large marcel waves of mousy hair. Such a loving smile, but unfortunately she had a club foot.

Auntie Cora made no trouble of it - nor anything else - she was always amicable and amused by the little ones.

Auntie Cora and the teacher served the meals, following which, the children would file back again to school. Little tummies full of casseroles, stews, pies and plenty of vegetables. Hot rice pudding, semolina, steamed fruit puddings with custard etc. When they had gone, Auntie Cora cleaned everywhere and washed up! After that she took off her cross-over apron, put on her cloche hat, long brown wool coat, and made her way back to the little cottage. There she lived with my grandfather Ulysses, his second wife Moira, and her mistress Aunt Fanny from the boarding house, who had all moved here away from the coastal bombing.

This demure lady was descended from the Russians. Her mother was a lady in waiting to the last Tzarina of Russia. Auntie Cora escaped with her mother, on the last ship to leave, at the time of the Revolution. Later all the Tzar's family was assassinated - so Auntie Cora left just in the nick of time!

Auntie Cora had once been asked to elope, but, refused, as she could not bear to leave her devoted Aunt Fanny, who had chosen her for a companion. He was a soldier in World War One, who was left waiting at night.

So Aunt Fanny and Auntie Cora lived in a Victorian boarding house by the sea in England. It was a place of excellence, before the War. In their dining room my mother and father first met. My father stayed there as a commercial traveller.

The rich velvet curtains, lace nets behind them, an aspidistra plant amongst the highly polished mahogany dining room suite, was the wonderful set, where my father wrote his orders. My young seventeen year old mother had walked in with a message for Aunt Fanny and my father never forgot her!

Many years later they were all together in this country village, called Willington, for the War. It is high up in the Chiltern Hills - very bracing!

Auntie Cora's experience at the boarding house - which was more like a hotel - was invaluable for her War effort of being the dinner lady for the school. They were very lucky to have her. She stayed until she was nearly eighty! The village children had all loved her - and were friends of hers as adults; and then sent their children! Very few knew she was Russian, and certainly would never have guessed she was brought up in the Tzar's palace! She escaped with coins sewn in the hem of her dress - which I now have, made up into a bracelet.

Chapter Four

The Village School

When the smell of powdery white chalk and bottled blue ink poured into open ink wells, hits my nose, it conjures up the dusty classroom and the teacher's chalky suits. The pupils used to flourish the duster around - full of blackboard chalk - powdering the nearby teacher, usually Miss Davis. Poor unfortunate Miss Davis! The larks they played on her were screamingly funny. We all laughed heartily and the poor distracted teacher tried to control us - without success. The boys never seemed to run out of ideas to entertain us. They were born comedians. The boys were always opening and shutting the tall window flap with a long pole, causing such hilarity.

The polished wood desks were in rows with an inkwell inserted in each. The children used to open their desk lids and giggle about behind them. Sometimes they chewed gum, and then stuck it in. They were large classrooms, high ceilinged, and painted dark green on the doors and panels round the walls. The wood floor planks were scrubbed and worn to a grey colour. The teacher's desk was raised so that she could oversee us but they still 'got away with murder'! It was like being in Will Hay's class, out of the film *Boys Will Be Boys*!'. One day two heavily built twin boys, who were always being really naughty - not having harmless fun - took objection to the frail headmaster. They picked him up, and threw him at the glass-panelled door. It broke with a loud crack, and he landed in the next classroom, bleeding badly. We were in the girls sewing class with a grandstand view of this, from the high-tiered benches of the assembly hall. We all jumped up horrified. One minute all quiet, so you could hear a pin drop - and then this crashing accident! My sweet angelic friend called Amber was frightened. I consoled her, and then a teacher appeared to cope with the situation. She then came back to us, who were sewing and chatting about what had happened, and said we could go home!

Joy – we put our things away and went out into the fair sunny afternoon; so refreshing since events had made us feel quite faint. Then the ambulance drew up and we were glad for our dear headmaster. It took him a long while to recover, and the twins were expelled.

A dashing copper-haired boy, with freckles, who always dressed smartly in expensive tweed suits, with cap to match, astounded the village school. He had impeccable manners, was very bright and earned high marks – his name was Kerry and he seemed beyond reproach. We girls thought he was very interesting! Then, one day, he took a pot shot at a passing train, with his father's rabbit gun: he wounded a man. We were stunned, and felt quite sick at the shock. He was sent away to a remand home.

Another afternoon a gang of the boys took it in turns to slash Carol and I all the way home with stinging nettles. They carried on doing this, so that by the time we arrived home we were covered in white sting spots! We did not mind very much and were really surprised when our parents were furious. Mine said that they'd had enough of this, and took me away from there. I protested as I liked all the excitement and fun – but they thought otherwise!

So Marie, my sister, and I, were sent to a convent down in the valley at a place called Dring. We had to walk miles and catch a bus, which was all right most of the time. It was, of course, quite different at the convent! We had different enjoyment and better education, but, we did so miss all the fun at our village school!

The village school was set on a triangle at the top crossroads, in quite a unique position. It was a strong Victorian building and very spacious and warm inside. I always looked forward to going there every morning – rain, snow or shine – and looked back on it full of nostalgia later.

I was too young to appreciate that my mother and father made great sacrifices for Marie and I to go to the convent for a good education. Now I really do, as we can join in all sorts of activities and enjoy all that we were taught, particularly when we have holidays abroad.

Chapter Five

Evacuees

Dark purple violets exude sweet scent that sends me drifting back to my little friend called Violet. She was an evacuee. They were children who had to evacuate their homes (or leave them, in other words) and live, for the duration of the War with another family in a house or on a farm. This was to provide safety away from the bombed towns.

Our evacuees came from London, only sixty miles away, but enough to be on the edge of the raids. Our country village was an ideal spot on the Chiltern Hills. Full of greenery, little cottages and a few grand homes on the outskirts. There were about six farms, dotted around, which provided such lovely scenes with the animals and the haymaking.

Many boys, who were staying here, helped my father with pea picking, potato picking and general jobs around our small holding. It was great fun when it was harvest festival and we all took wheelbarrows full of giant marrows, apples, vegetables and salad, tomatoes, flowers and oats, barley, corn and wheatsheaves. We trundled up the village, with various bits falling off on the way, and the laughter rang out as we retrieved it. Then we arrived at the little low church all dark, cold and echoey and we rolled the barrows in from the brilliant hot sunshine. The change was such a contrast, and we would blink to see, then, when we became accustomed to the dark we would start putting everything around in the right places, Dad's giant marrow always in the middle on the steps before the alter.

One evening in the winter of 1940, all the evacuees came to the chapel hall (where the school dinners were served normally) for a concert. We were encouraged to join in 'run, rabbit, run rabbit, run, run, run' – which included words about Hitler!

We all became more friendly singing together – and all the patriotic songs made us feel brave and ready to conquer Hitler at any cost! There was the cockney drawl and the rich Hertfordshire brogue blending together – it was funny – besides our London King's English, and some Irish, Jewish and a few from the north. We were a real mixture and it was wonderful being all comrades together. Life was austere but great in friendship. We were all in it together and on a level; rationing for food, clothing and petrol was equal for everyone. Everyone was so pally. When you got on a bus, there were smiles all round, and the bus driver would stop in all sorts of places to be helpful!

Further along our road, by about three miles was a famous nature cure home. Residents from there would pass by our gate, and I saw many famous film stars, and theatre stars. I was lucky to have that place included in my round for collecting red cross donations. They would be swanning around in thick white towels, sipping carrot juice! This was quite unheard of then and the whole atmosphere was unusually Hollywood set style!

The notice of 'careless talk costs lives' was hung up all over the place – in buses, cafés and cinemas. The buses had sticky tape criss-crossed over the windows to stop bomb blast – just in case, and the same applied to the cafés and so on, because every where the public would chat could lead to the giving away of vital information to spies in disguise.

We were all so close in helping one another recover, and everyone over the age of eighteen had to join up to the forces, munitions factories, land army or civil defence. We were all in one common cause – to overthrow the enemy.

Evacuees and ourselves were all asked to 'make do and mend' and we went to it with a will! It gave us the chance to renovate and make something for best. Dresses had inserts, trousers had patches, but all very carefully and tastefully done. Long after the War, these ideas became high fashion – patches were actually put on to be trendy even when not needed! The blanket stitched patches are very fashionable now in sweaters – and look really good. Back in the War we were doubtful about appearing in them at first – but 'when needs must' – only to find it was attractive.

Violet was as bouncy as her bouncy ball games, we played together against the wall of our bungalow, in the dreamy late summer evenings. We played for hours, doing all the latest twists and turns we could before catching it. Her gleaming straight hair, cut in a bob, flew up and down as she caught the ball. Her bright pale mauve eyes smiling away at me as we played. We were always content together; the hours raced by.

One evacuee was crying one day by the bushes. Her tears splashed down as she shook the leaves distractedly. I asked her what was wrong, and she replied

"My father's in the desert, and he's only allowed one tumbler full of water per day- either to wash with or drink. It must be terrible!"

I was stunned –one only to wash or drink! Those poor desert rats did suffer when the Battle of El Alemain under Mounty, was on. But it was worth it, we got through!

In summer we played with evacuees along the lanes, or in the garden. Lovely flowers all round, cowslips and yarrow along the hedgerows and fluffy yellow honeysuckle and brambles over the hedges. The scent was glorious. In the winter we played snowballs, when we had freezing cold times. The snow was as high as the small trees and sometimes formed a tunnel. It was as pretty as fairyland – but our toes and fingers were bitterly cold! Snowballs would cling on to our wobbly hats and freeze there. Snowmen stood for a week after being made, before melting. Our winters were long and hard –the rain or sleet would sting with the force of the drive – but, then, when it was spring it really was spring. There were definite seasons then – so you could expect to be warm in spring, and positively hot in the summer.

I remember once I went under the strawberry nets in the summer, when a German plane flew over. He was the only one I saw all the War – but he came very low – I was terrified – I could see him in the cockpit looking at me. I squashed my face in the mud and prayed. Then he swooped off – thank goodness! We were so lucky to be away from the bombing and usual dread of German aeroplanes. This I thought as I disentangled myself from the strawberry nets, and picked off the straw which covers them also, (hence the name strawberries, which I never knew until I lived in the country). How providential that the one who flew over our village was a thoughtful airman. So, our evacuees were safe again and we were all together in our little retreat!

Chapter Six

Sweets

A dab of hard toffee stuck into the fizzy white powder called sherbet, was tuppence worth of bliss! Those bags of sherbet dabs, that were so popular then, bring back wonderful taste buds on the tongue! Effervescent joy – with the strong toffee lollipops inside, was a dream to look forward to on a Saturday morning trip to the village sweet shop.

Clutching a few pennies and our sweet coupons, we skipped along the gravel road. Plenty of time on a Saturday! No school, and later we could be in our play houses our father had built for Marie and I. Concrete floors, dark green painted door and windows and all made from rustic reject pit props, including a pretty porch to each. My mother would let us take our dinners in them to eat on our own, for a treat. I loved that! The cream plate with my favourite corned beef, mashed potato and tangy home-made chutney – which I had helped to make together with all sorts of other lovely dinners that my mother made especially well, were taken in there; gorgeous rabbit pie with carrots, sausages and mash, stews with all sorts of vegetables including swede. Lovely sweets – desserts – followed. Steaming hot rice pudding with a golden 'skin' on the top – steamed canary pudding and custard, queen of puddings, apple charlotte, spotted dog, jam roly-poly, blackberry and apple, cold fresh fruit salad. Mum made the simplest dish taste heavenly!

All around the garden and on the land, were our pets, including two black shiny coated Labradors – that got into mischief with the neighbouring farmer's cows and pigs! We had three cats, white, black and white and ginger. Once we had three kittens – a ginger and two tabbies: the two pet rabbits, Thumpa and Bumpa, liked to be carried in a little cart Dad made, attached by braid harness to our smaller ginger and white wavy-haired dog called Chips. Round and round they went, over the bumps, and loved it!

They just looked straight ahead with their big navy blue eyes very solemnly and made us roar with laughter. They never attempted to jump out! They were Dutch with white silky hair with large blobs of bluey black on them – like ink blots! We loved them, and kept them well supplied with heaps of dandelion leaves and carrots. There was also a tiny bluey grey rabbit called Blue Peter, with pale blue eyes – so gentle and tame that he hopped around the lawn with us.

Back home from the sweetshop we would arrange our fondant letter sweets to form names, put brown lozengers out for the doll's 'beef' dinner, and suck lemon crystals intended really for the drink! Chewing gum and bubble gum (introduced by the yanks) was rather frowned on – but, the one to which all of our parents objected was the large, single sweet called a gobstopper! It was a ball shape and stretched the mouth to horrible proportions, and could have choked us! The attraction to us was that, as each layer dissolved of the sugary coating, it turned into another colour. This prompted us to keep taking it out to look and see!

The tiny old cottage sweet shop had a window of small squared panes, yellow with dusty age, and torn grey net curtains dangling about, so that one could neither see in nor out! It held great intrigue for we children were of an age where cleanliness is not a priority choice. Ours was of the sweet selection! Here was a paradise for sweet-toothed people! Row upon row of glass jars full of rainbow colours and varying shapes. Around the two small counters, open boxes of sweets, such as liquorice laces, pipes and Catherine wheels, sherbet fountains, rhubarb sticks, barley sugar twists, gobstoppers and chewing gums were laid. As you entered the 'dungeon' type place, you stepped down two stone steps, onto the flag stone floor. In front and at the side of you, by the window (that shed no light), were all the sweets. Winter mixtures and fruit salad in jars, brown lozenges, aniseed balls, Pontefract-cakes, toasted coconut, marsh mallows, rainbow nibs, black treacle toffee and on and on! The bell attached to the top of the door clanged to announce our arrival, but Mrs Grundy did not appear. Usually the short, plump beaproned lady, with a brown 'bun' on top of her head, burst through a dirty flowered curtain from the back to serve us. She was short-sighted, and peered through her steel-rimmed glasses to dive into the big jars. We waited and waited – then we heard a rustle.

We shuffled from one foot to another on the cold floor, when suddenly we saw a brown mouse nibbling a big cheese on the grocery part of the counter! He was running about in the bacon slicer! We froze – we felt sick – should we wait for the gobstoppers? It moved again – and we all shrieked and ran out of the shop 'post-haste'! The pull was great – but that put a stopper to our gobstoppers!

Chapter Seven

The Spy

The sight of an old crumpled stone raincoat, or an old black bowler hat - sends shivers down my spine! These were worn by tall Mr Kreep. His shifty eyes darted about behind his half shaped steel rimmed glasses. He carried a briefcase and walked stiffly - like a War time spy we thought.

Why wasn't he in the forces? A farmer, a factory worker or something? Very suspicious! We whispered about him, to one another, in huddles. He was a loner, who lived in the hut of a remote field, and nobody seemed to know who he was or what he did. If he saw anyone approaching he would dash inside his hut. He never went in the village shops and yet was seen reading a newspaper! Where did he buy his food?

One day he came out all dressed in his best pinstriped suit, flower in the buttonhole, polished light brown shoes and starched white collar. We were excited. Something was going to happen!

We crouched in the bushes and watched. Out came his Jack Russell dog, followed by five puppies! They were cute, all romping around. Suddenly Mr Kreep held his hand over his eye (the glasses were not on that day). He muttered angrily and fumbled about in the grass. Then he fetched a stick, and swished that in the field grass. He whistled to the dogs to go in, and in they all scampered. We waited; nothing happened. The rain fell and we got soaked, so we had to go home.

A few days later, whilst waiting in the queue at the post office, someone said,

"That theerr maan, 'oo lives in theerr hut, was getting married in theerr week - but one of 'ees puppies swallowed his false eye and, that put ar stop t'that! Neverr turned up, 'ee did! His la-di-da girl friend, called Poppy (she looked like a bright red poppy, did 'err face too)

too) was left crying! 'Ee retrieved the false eye later, apparently! Never married 'err though."

Some escape, we thought, from a so-called spy!

Chapter Eight

Dad's Friend

Mr Mowe was a tall man, dressed in tweeds with a waistcoat, and plucked a fresh straw for his hat every morning. This was stuck in the band, and taken out and chewed every now and then. This golden straw wobbled about in his mouth as he talked, adding to his engaging grin. He was 'up with the lark' literally, starting his morning round of jobs long before breakfast. Then he ate heartily and strolled round to us. He would lean on the window sill of our bow window, pontificating, whilst we laughed at him over breakfast. It was a great start to the day, especially when accompanied by the donkey, Neddy. He would sometimes poke his nose in, too, and add to the merriment. You could hear his hooves clipping and scraping on the rocks of our rockery below the window! Everything grew easily there, as it was very fertile ground, so it didn't matter, and in any case, even if it did spoil the plants, it was worth it for the love of that donkey.

Neddy had been neglected by the previous owner, and now Dad and Mr Mowe shared him. If you patted him a cloud of dust went up! They soon got him well groomed and he became less timid and so gentle.

Mr Mowe was a knowledgeable man of country life. He knew all about animals; and did everything you can think of for the community, even down to being the village undertaker! Dad and he got on very well, as not only did their personalities blend, but, they were both such hard workers. They both had a good sense of humour and would laugh a lot together.

Mr Mowe helped Dad with his horses frequently. The only trouble was once with the handsome hunter, Bobby! Mr Mowe was giving instructions on how to break him in, where they have to trot round in a circle on a heavy rope, to your commands but Bobby objected to this, and even more so, when Mr Mowe was directing

Bobby. He threw his front legs up in the air, prancing around and caught Dad's mouth and kicked most of his teeth out! Dad came running in with a hanky over his mouth and attempted to ask Mum for the keys to his car. He drove down to the dentist, who took them out. Dad's great ambition was to own horses. Even as a little boy, of Old Kent Road, in London, he used to pretend the end of his bed was a horse and cart! His mother was always catching him! She was warm-hearted, and hoped he would have a horse one day. Now he had four. Algernon (Algey for short) was a sixteen hand palomino, who pulled our wagonette - a grand effort in very dark green, and was a six-seater. We would be going along fine, when he would stop for a rest - as he was old; and fall down on his leather knee pads to be comfortable. Everybody used to laugh, and after five minutes off he would go again!

Whether the news of the War was bad or good we were always busy and cheerful, everyone in the village was. Even the ones with grumpy looking faces were really full of fun when they spoke. One of the amazing things that happened, concerned one very jolly lady, who was also very fat (but nobody minded in those days). She used to ride up and down to the village quite a long way each day on her bike. Sue was the post lady, and a really important person in our lives. One day she didn't appear, nor the next and so on, so I enquired, thinking perhaps she was on holiday with her husband 'home on leave'.

"No" was the reply, "she has had a baby, but didn't know because of her usual size." I couldn't believe it - but it was true. She told me next time she was out - just the same size, on that tiny saddle! She had waited for twelve years, and given up hope, so she couldn't understand it when her baby boy was born! I saw him a few years later - the image of her, on his toy bike. We went out on horses or bikes. Dandy pulled the cart, Kitty and Bessie took saddle rides. Bessie was from a circus and would only ride round in a circle. She had a broad back for the bareback riders and looked so beautiful all white with a cream mane and tail - but she had to go, as we could not get her to go along the lanes; just turning and turning as if in the ring! Kitty was a fluffy-haired black, cuddly looking pony. She would do anything and was very obedient.

Dad and Mr Mowe built twenty hutches for the rabbits, and a long run for the new bunnies. Also, they built a large chicken coop and a run for the new chicks. These were all out of rustic split trunks with the bark showing, like the other buildings, which looked so attractive.

They made garden seats, bird houses, gates and all sorts, out of the legal reject pit props. All other wood was not allowed in the War, as it was all needed for essential help, as there were so few timber men – they had all gone to the War.

In the stables, all rustic outside, the horses smelt wonderful, and champed their bits and rattled their harness when getting ready to go out. They whinnied with delight and then enjoy their trotting. Once home they steamed in the stables as they ate their hay, from the bracket on the wall. Dad and Mr Mowe cleaned the leather harness with saddle soap and polish, and shone up the brasses. The saddles were hung up on hooks, with hay bags. Dad's eyes smiled with happiness at them. No wonder he had always wanted horses – they are such wonderful sights and have such wonderful smells. We all helped clearing out the animals and leaving them fresh straw. We walked the dogs, and stroked the cats and rabbits. Only a short while before, in London, we had no inkling we would be doing all this so soon. We just had one lovely black cat there called Timmy. He died there before we left, he was about twelve years old. Just as well for him, as it would have been such a change when he was older, and he might have badly missed his old patch.

Mr Mowe would collect fresh apples off his tree and give plenty to the horses and donkey. His wife baked superb cakes and pies, and the aroma of which floated over that pretty, high-banked corner where they lived. Everything – as they say – in apple pie order.

My sweet friend Amber, who also went to the village school with me every morning, was Mr and Mrs Mowe's granddaughter. She was cosseted because of her frail health, but was of such placid, strong disposition, not wanting all the attention herself. They obviously must have known the situation, because she died of a brain tumour just after the end of the War. Amber had always longed for her black and white, whispy-haired, gentle mongrel Patsie to have puppies. All the War passed with none; the week she died Patsie had four puppies – which she never saw. How I cried for her.

Chapter Nine

Christmas

Christmas was still celebrated even in the War. Still the stars reminded us of Bethlehem's star on the night Jesus was born. They twinkled away like diamonds on black velvet in the night sky. The same stars were looked at the world over – even by the servicemen and the home fire burners!

On Christmas Day there was a cease fire, on the front line especially – the men of both sides came out and shook hands!

The servicemen had parcels from home, and letters were read avidly.

At home everyone dressed in their best, went to church and prayed for peace, and all those who were caught up in the War. Then back home to undo the parcels under the Christmas tree. These were not as plentiful nor generous as pre-War but nevertheless very exciting to have a gift at all. The actual tree was not as splendid either – most often just big branches of a fir type tree – but they were decorated with all the old baubles, tinsel, fairy etc., and home-made craft inventions that were very good. The whole lounge was draped with new paper chains that Marie and I made for hours beforehand – like most children. All the old decorations came out as well, and everyone enjoyed decking their homes with bells, trumpets, paper twists, holly and mistletoe.

We went carol singing before it was too dark, as no torches or lamps must be shown after dark, because of the blackout. It was as pretty as ever when the snow or ice lay on the ground. If it was an orange sunset, the beautiful colour glowed over the country scene.

Christmas dinner was as near as possible to the real thing. Mothers saved and made marvellous dinners to celebrate on the day. We had roast chicken every year, from our own brood, all our own fresh vegetables, bread sauce, thick gravy and any extras like chipolatas or belly of pork if the butcher had any that year. Mum managed to make a Christmas pudding and white sauce, or brandy if Dad had any. We lit it with the holly on top one time, and the holly burnt of course! What a laugh.

One Christmas I was in trouble! I had been given a joke plate wobbler for a present. I decided to try it out on my ultra smart Auntie Sophia. I pumped it up too fast, and the boiling hot soup fell in her lap! She jumped up screaming and it was all over her expensive outfit! I was severely told off – we made Auntie comfortable – and then we all went on to enjoy Dad's wonderful jokes again. He was always the life and soul of the party. He had served in world War One and was badly injured but never lost his sense of humour.

We all washed up together, then had a snooze in the darkening room by the fire. We played with our new toys whilst the grown ups had tea. Then we always played charades! We went to no end of trouble – dressing up and planning it all for ages – with our cousins, or whoever was staying for Christmas. Then it was time for Hands Off And Eyes On – a white sheet over some of the team whilst the others hid, then the opposing team had to guess how many were under there – with no touching, only using the eyes. Up to the big dining room table for supper – cold meat and salad, or pickles, with bread and 'scrape'! Then the table would be cleared for board games and tippet – my father being hilarious again. Worn out with laughing we would tumble into bed. Our bunk beds were made from huge wood beams, which Dad found, and built into the extension at the back. Wide and cosy, but the room was bitterly cold. We used to lie under the covers and take twelve 'breaths' by which time you were supposed to be warm! Mum was marvellous though, and if it was really cold we could put coats on the top, and share the one stone hot water bottle (I used to get terrible chilblains – possibly from this – but, then, a lot of us did.)

Our teeth chattering with cold on a Christmas night, we would concentrate on the lovely events of the day. Nativity at church, presents, dinner, giggling games, and possibly my funny, witty Uncle Bill doing conjuring tricks! The aunties all dressed with lacey trims and smelt of perfume, with their hair shining and curled, with the usual bandeau or snoods pulled on! I revelled in company, and loved having the relatives come to stay.

Boxing day we all went for walks, after feeding and tending the animals. We looked over our new toys again and wrote some thank you letters. Dad's newly invented games came out and we had lovely fun again with him. We huddled by the courtier stove and read books. The radio was turned on for some well known entertaining programme. The best of these was Itma short for 'It's That Man Again' - Tommy Handley coming over the waves with Mrs Mop and the Diver! Their jokes were talked about all the week, every week, wherever you went. The Premier's speeches and Itma were always topical!

Christmas is the most lovely, hospitable time of the year, celebrating the birth of Jesus - and it brings with it a whole lot more besides. The recognition of love in the family, which we remember forever, especially when it is cold outside and we are warm together inside. I fall asleep thinking 'Oh, Jesus, I'm glad you were born!'

Chapter Ten

Sunday Afternoons

In deep winter, Sunday afternoons were pleasantly spent water-colour painting, with Dad. He was very talented at this, as well as his carpentry.

Dad, Marie and I sat at the large Jacobean table, with newspaper. All the paint boxes were out - and there were many, as we were all keen, paper of all kinds, jars of water with brushes, and rags to mop up.

Marie's paintings were emerging - but her later ones of VE Day (victory in Europe day, may 8th 1945) were remarkable, which, of course, we did not know about as yet. All those celebrations were exultant in every street throughout great Britain. Up went the bunting, flags everywhere - the famous red, white and blue of the great Union Jack! Everyone burst with joy - except the poor sad ones who had lost those so close to them. Even some of those managed to join in bravely. Winston Churchill was so elated with all the British - saying it was our 'finest hour'! This was indeed how we all felt, and he so eloquently phrased it for us. Parties and bonfires happened all over the place!

For years, earlier, we sat and painted, where my ambition to go to an art school was born. My father let me after I left school, for two years. It was an incredibly happy time. It was peace, and I met my boyfriend who I married five years later! He would laugh at my arty smocks and tam-o'-shanter berets, that I wore on the 'bus!

My father taught us many interesting details about how to paint, so the hours would slip by, whilst Mum and Auntie Beckie would have a rest. This was the only rest my mother had all the week. She was busy with all the housework, cooking and working on the land.

My poor mother lost her treasured gold wedding ring in the potato field! We never did find it. She was most distressed. Dad had to buy another one from Dring – but, it was not the same for her, of course. She worked so hard, her hand must have become slimmer and it fell off and disappeared into the wet soil. I sometimes wonder if anyone found it. It would have meant so much to her, but some people would think it would not matter. My father and mother were a unique couple – they had such high standards, so loveable, and were very good looking. They both achieved so much in their life time, it is hard to comprehend. They had excellent taste in furnishings and kept a delightful home. Many of the unusual ornaments coming from my father's future fancy goods and ironmongers shop. The heavy expensive furniture having been designed by my father for when they were married!

His dexterity was apparent in his paintings, and their sheer joy of living was expressed in both my mother's and my father's art. Both also wrote prolifically – my mother with her correspondence to friends and relatives, and my father in his book, *An Untaxed Millionaire*, meaning how the best things in life are free.

The colours and hues splashed over the paper, and we dabbled with our brushes. Lovely days of childhood, so special to us.